M000014316

Look Out, Mack!

by Dot Meharry
illustrated by Ian Forss

Harcourt
SCHOOL PUBLISHERS

Printed in China

ISBN 10: 0-15-350340-8
ISBN 13: 978-0-15-350340-5

Ordering Options
ISBN 10: 0-15-350331-9 (Grade 1 Below-Level Collection)
ISBN 13: 978-0-15-350331-3 (Grade 1 Below-Level Collection)
ISBN 10: 0-15-357391-0 (package of 5)
ISBN 13: 978-0-15-357391-0 (package of 5)

5 6 7 8 9 10   468   15 14 13 12 11 10 09

Look at Mack.

He is so fast.

Look out, Mack!

Oh, no!
It is too late.

Look at Jack.

Can Jack help?

Yes!